Alisa's First Adventure

Written by Liz Ball

Illustrated by Bree Stallings

Alisa's First Adventure

Published by Tree Farm Press
Williamston, MI 48895 USA

ISBN: 978-0-692-18141-6 (paperback)
ISBN: 978-0-692-18142-3 (ebook)
LCCN: 2018956419

To my dad:

"Thanks for always believing in me."

Alisa sat by the big oak tree;
little tears fell down her cheeks.
She was so very sad.

The wind blew softly,
and the sun smiled
down on her face,
but Alisa was still sad.

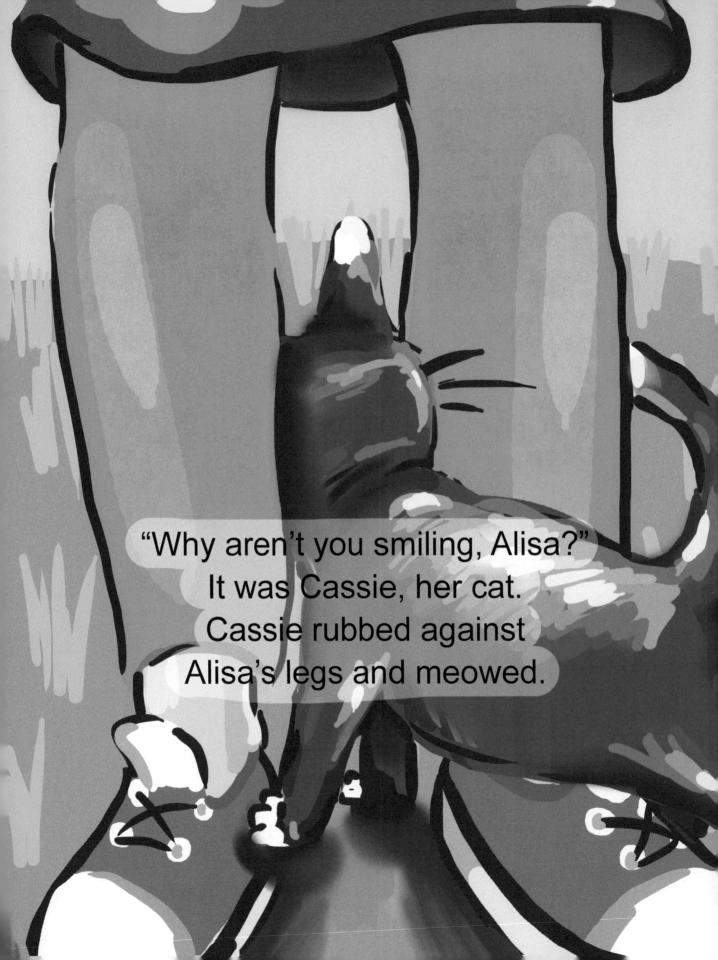

"Why aren't you smiling, Alisa?"
It was Cassie, her cat.
Cassie rubbed against
Alisa's legs and meowed.

Alisa followed Cassie towards the big oak tree. Cassie reached her front paws up to the lowest branch and hung. Alisa followed her lead.

Cassie showed Alisa how to pull one foot up over the branch and swing one leg around until she was sitting on the branch.

Soon, Alisa was climbing ahead of Cassie, laughing, until they reached the very top of the tree.

Sitting on the highest branch,
Alisa felt big and grown up.
Cassie jumped on her lap,
purring in agreement.

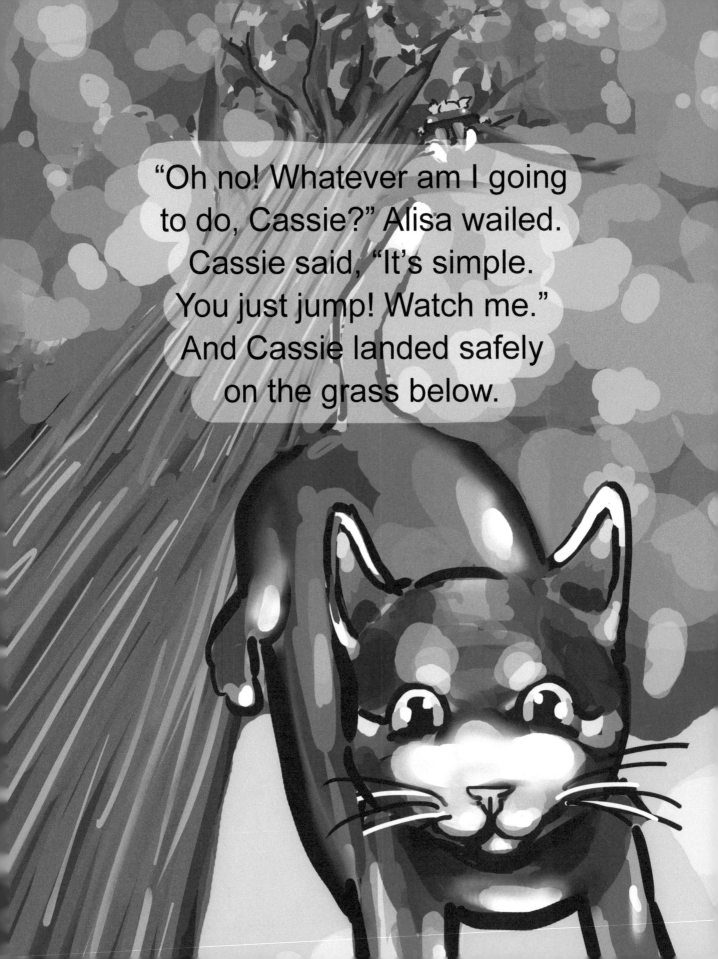

Cassie thought a minute.
Realizing that Alisa was right,
she meowed and ran off.
Now Alisa felt very alone and small.
"How will I ever get down?"

Moments later, Alisa's dad stood beneath the tree with Cassie sitting by his feet. He laughed. "Honey, it's okay. I'll catch you. Just jump."

Alisa stared down at her big, strong dad. She closed her eyes and counted to three.

"No more climbing for you...
at least not for a while.
Now, let's go eat," her dad said.

CPSIA information can be obtained
at www.ICGtesting.com
Printed in the USA
LVHW07n2258190918
590750LV00003B/3/P